My Holiday in

France

Susie Brooks

WAYLAND

First published in 2008 by Wayland

Copyright © Wayland 2008

Wayland
338 Euston Road
London NW1 3BH

Wayland Australia
Level 17/207 Kent Street
Sydney NSW 2000

Senior Editor: Claire Shanahan
Designer: Elaine Wilkinson
Map artwork: David le Jars

Brooks, Susie
My holiday in France
1. Vacations - France - Juvenile literature 2. Recreation -
France - Juvenile literature 3. France - Juvenile
literature 4. France - Social life and customs - 21st
century - Juvenile literature I. Title II. France
914.4'0484

ISBN 978 0 7502 5326 0

Cover: Eiffel Tower © Free Agents Limited/Corbis; Snowboarder near Mont Blanc © David Spurdens/Corbis.

p5: © qaphotos.com/Alamy; p6: © Roy Rainford/Robert Harding World Imagery/Corbis; p7: © David
Spurdens/Corbis; p8: © Lourens Smak/Alamy; p9: © Bruno Barbier/Robert Harding World Imagery/Corbis; p10: ©
G. Bowater/Corbis; p11: © Wayland Picture Library; p12: © Free Agents Limited/Corbis; p13: © Paul
Almasy/Corbis; © Owen Franken/Corbis; © Wayland; © Katie Powell; p14: © AFP/Getty Images; p15: © Durand
Patrick/Corbis Sygma; p16: © Ted Spiegel/Corbis; p17: Geoffrey Clements/Corbis; p18: © Owen Franken/Corbis;
p19 © Tom Brakefield/Corbis; p20: © James Quigley/Getty; p21: © Wayland Picture Library; p22: © Chev
Wilkinson/Getty; p23: © AFP/Getty Images: ©; p24: © Bernard Annebicque/Corbis Sygma; p25: © Getty Images;
p26, title page: © Schlegelmilch/Corbis; p27: ©; ©; p28: © Reuters/Corbis; p29: © Jeff
Vespa/Contributor/Getty.

Printed in China

Wayland is a division of Hachette Children's Books, an Hachette Livre UK company.

www.hachettelivre.co.uk

Contents

This is France!

France is a big country in western Europe. Many people who come here on holiday fly to Paris, the capital city.

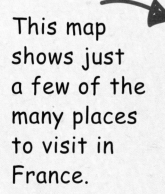

This map shows just a few of the many places to visit in France.

From the UK, you can take a train through the Channel Tunnel under the sea! There are ferries that go to France, too.

On a Channel Tunnel train, you can't tell you are deep under water!

It was exciting arriving in France, but I couldn't understand what people were saying!

Speak French!

hello
bonjour (bon-**j**hor)

thank you
merci (mair-**see**)

please
s'il vous plait (see-voo-**plai**)

5

Sunshine and snow

France is a good place to visit for warm summer weather. Lots of people head for the sunny beaches in the south of the country.

River swimming under the Pont du Gard bridge is fun on a hot summer's day.

Speak French!

sun
soleil (sol-ay)

snow
niege (nee-ehj)

beach
plage (plahje)

Winter brings people to the mountains for skiing and other snow sports. It is cold on the slopes, but the sun is still very strong.

This snowboarder is in the Alps, near France's highest mountain, Mont Blanc.

I put on so much suncream my nose was white – it looked funny but I didn't get burnt.

Somewhere to sleep

France is famous for its **chateaux**, like this one in the Loire Valley.

People who visit French cities and seaside towns usually stay in hotels or **apartments**. In the countryside, your bed could be in a cottage – or a castle!

Houseboats are popular in France – there are beds inside.

Some people rent holiday homes called gites. In the mountains, you might stay in a **chalet**. Camping is fun if you like an adventure and the weather is good.

Speak French!

bedroom
chambre (shom-bre)

bathroom
salle de bain (sal-de-ban)

shower
douche (doosh)

Whizzing around

France has some of the fastest trains in the world. Travelling from city to city by train is usually much quicker than going by car.

TGV trains speed along at up to 300 kilometres per hour!

There are plenty of free cycle paths in France. This one is near a river.

If you want to enjoy the scenery in France, go on a bike ride. Cycle along a river – there will be lots to see and hopefully not many hills!

On French roads

- People drive on the right-hand side of the road.
- You can't travel in the front of a car until you are 10.
- Drivers have to pay to use most motorways.

Action-packed Paris

This is the Eiffel Tower. You can take a lift right to the top.

No one gets bored in Paris! France's capital city is famous for its art, fashion and impressive buildings.

While you're here...

Pick your favourite picture inside the Louvre...

and the Pompidou Centre art galleries.

Spot the funny **gargoyles** on Notre Dame Cathedral.

Play or watch a puppet show in one of the city parks.

Take a ride on...

- a **carousel** in the Tuileries gardens
- a boat along the River Seine
- an underground **Metro** train – count the stops!

13

Great days out

Don't miss these places just outside Paris.

Meet the characters at Parc Asterix before you go on all the rides.

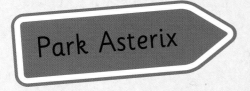
Park Asterix

A fun park based on France's favourite comic book hero Asterix and his friend Obelix.

We had a day at Euro Disney – I wanted to go on all the rides, but there wasn't time!

Look out for:
- The Hall of Mirrors
- The Neptune and Dragon fountains
- Rowing boats and a mini-train.

France Miniature

Visit France Miniature to see famous places toy-sized! Paris's Arc de Triomphe looks tiny here.

Speak French!

garden
jardin (jhar-da)

ticket
billet (bee-yay)

park
parc (park)

15

Northern sights

Go to see the Bayeux tapestry. It's like a giant comic strip!

A little further from Paris, but within easy reach, are more popular sights. Every year, thousands of people visit Mont St Michel – a magical abbey on a rock in the sea.

A trip to Giverny shows you France through an artist's eyes. This was the home of Monet, one of the country's best-known painters.

Look for Monet's bridge and water lilies in the garden at Giverny.

Paint like Monet!

- Use blobs of bright colours.
- Paint flowers, fields or the seaside.
- Paint in different weathers.

17

Journeying south

Many people go on driving holidays through France. Travelling south from Paris, here are some things you might see.

Thick forests full of wildlife

People picking grapes to make wine

Fields of bright yellow sunflowers

Wild, white horses in the marshy **Camargue**

 Castles and bridges made of sand-coloured stone

 Purple fields of lavender

 The Pyrenees Mountains

The great aquarium at La Rochelle, on the west coast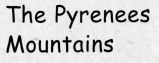

 The Mediterranean Sea

Tasty treats

In France, you will always find good things to eat. There is a huge choice of cheeses, meats, fruits, cakes and pastries.

Take a picnic to the park, with a basket of bread, pâté, grapes and salami.

Dad's favourite food was snails – yuck! They were really chewy and tasted of garlic!

CRÉPES SUCRÉES
SUCRE   2
CONFITURE   2
CHOCOLAT   3
BEURRE   3
RHUM   4
GRAND MARNIER 5

Eating in cafés is popular in French cities. You can often sit outside. Crusty bread is served with every meal.

Don't forget to try a pancake, called a crêpe, in France.

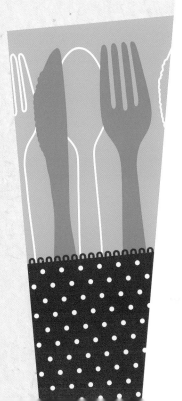

On the menu

baguette (bag-**ett**) - **a stick of bread**

fromage (from-**ah**-je) - **cheese**

boisson (bwa-son) - **drink**

Time to shop

France has some enormous supermarkets, but it can be more fun to buy your food in an open-air market or small local shop.

Patisseries like this one have mouth-watering displays.

The money people spend in France is called the euro.

The city of Strasbourg has a popular market at Christmas time.

French cities are famous for their small, smart shops called boutiques. Look for **souvenirs** to take home, such as lace from **Normandy** or pottery from **Provence**.

Speak French!

bakery
boulangerie (boo-**lon**-jair-ee)

cake shop
patisserie (pat-**ee**-sair-ee)

newsagent
tabac (tab-ack)

23

Being French

When you visit France, you'll learn a bit about how the French people live. You might notice different traditions around the country.

In the boggy Landes region, shepherds used to walk on stilts like these local dancers.

There are many different religions in France. **Roman Catholics** are the biggest group. They worship in beautiful churches and cathedrals.

Millions of Roman Catholics visit the holy town of Lourdes every year, to pray or help people in need.

When I met my French cousins, they kissed me on both cheeks!

Speak French!

mother
mère (maire)

father
père (paire)

sister
sœur (sur)

brother
frère (fraire)

Ready to play

Many people visit France to see big sports events. The Tour de France is a huge cycling race. At Le Mans and Monaco, there is famous motor racing.

The Monaco Grand Prix is a daring race around twisty streets!

Other popular sports include soccer (football), rugby and **boules**. On the coasts you can swim, windsurf and even sail yachts across the sand.

In boules, you have to roll your ball as close to the little marker ball as you can.

At the Tour de France, people write the names of their favourite cyclists on the road.

Festival fever

Being in France on 14 July means being at a party! This is **Bastille Day**, France's biggest festival. Look out for fireworks, flags and loud marching bands.

A famous Bastille Day parade marches through the Arc de Triomphe in Paris.

Many regions have their own festivals. The city of Cannes hosts a huge film festival every year, when stars come from all over the world.

A big red carpet is laid out for the stars at Cannes. Not many people are lucky enough to go!

Party places

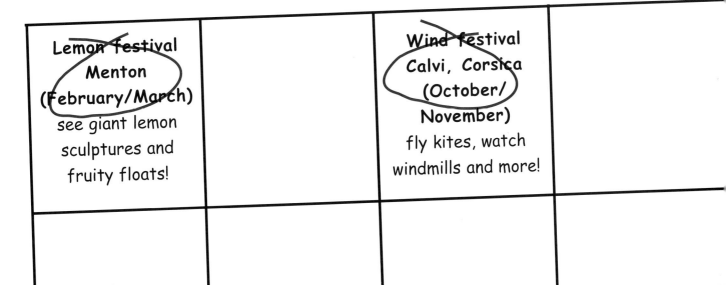

Lemon festival Menton (February/March) see giant lemon sculptures and fruity floats!		Wind festival Calvi, Corsica (October/ November) fly kites, watch windmills and more!	

Make it yourself

France has a crêpe for everyone. Make these and find your favourite flavour!

Crêpes

1. Ask an adult to cook or heat up the pancakes. Stack them with pieces of foil or greaseproof paper between them so they don't stick together.

2. Experiment with different yummy toppings! Try the ideas on the opposite page.

Sweet

- Chocolate spread and banana
- Lemon juice with sugar or hundreds and thousands
- Strawberry jam and vanilla ice cream

Savoury

- Cheese and ham (heat this up again to melt the cheese)
- Cream cheese and chopped tomatoes
- Ratatouille (a cooked vegetable mix)

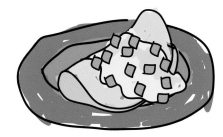

TIP: Try serving your crêpes in different ways – folded, rolled, or even piled up with fillings in between!

Useful words

apartment
: A room or flat for living in.

Bastille Day
: A national holiday celebrating an important battle of 1789.

boules
: A game where people roll metal balls along the ground.

Camargue
: A marshy plain in the south of France.

carousel
: A merry-go-round.

chalet
: A type of wooden house, common in the Alps.

chateau (plural chateaux)
: A French castle.

gargoyle
: A waterspout carved in the shape of a strange figure.

Metro
: The underground train system in Paris.

Normandy
: A region in north-west France.

Provence
: A region in south-east France.

Roman Catholic
: A type of Christian.

souvenir
: Something you take home to remind you of somewhere you have been.